MW01242837

Maid For Me

THE BILLIONAIRE'S MAID SERIES, BOOK THREE

DAWN SULLIVAN

All rights reserved. No part of this publication may be reproduced, stored in a retrieval system, or transmitted in any form or by means of mechanical, electronic, photocopying, recording, or otherwise, without prior permission from the author. This is a work of fiction. Names, characters, places, and events are fictitious in every regard. Any similarities to actual events or persons, living or dead, are purely coincidental. Any trademarks, service marks, product names, or featured names are assumed to be the property of their respective owners and are used only for reference. There is no implied endorsement of any of these terms used. Except for review purposes, the reproduction of this book in whole or in part, mechanically or electronically, constitutes a copyright violation. Published in the United States of America on November 2021; Copyright 2021 by Dawn Sullivan. The right of the Author's Name to be identified as the Author of the Work has been asserted by them in accordance with The Copyright, Designs, and Patent Act of 1988.

Published by Dawn Sullivan

Cover Design: KL Fast

Edited by: Ryder Editing and Formatting

Copyright 2021 © Author Dawn Sullivan

Language: English

❀ Created with Vellum

For Tabitha and Karrie. You two are absolutely amazing! Thank you so much for all that you do for me!

Gabriella

When I came home to help keep my mother's cleaning business afloat after she became ill, I had no idea what I was getting myself into. Nothing prepared me for him. Jameson Hughes. I knew who he was. Everyone did. The hotshot music producer who had landed my favorite rock band, Rebellious Dynasty, when I was a teenager. I had stalked him back then almost as much as I followed the band. While others were mooning over the rockstars, I was stuck on their producer with his piercing, dark eyes, strong jawline, and a mouth I wanted to explore with my own. A man I desired even more now, even though I shouldn't. I was there to help my mother, and then I was going back to New York... wasn't I?

Jameson

From the moment I saw Gabriella Reyes, I wanted her. I craved her like no other. Her wide, innocent eyes and luscious curves drew me in, while her beautiful voice had me clinging to every lyric she sang. As owner of a multi-billion dollar recording studio, I should have been fighting to get her to sign with me, but instead I found I wanted to keep her all to myself. The more I got to know her, one thing became clear. She was made for me, my favorite melody, and I wasn't letting her go.

Dawn Sullivan

I sat in a chair next to the hospital bed, my head bowed, my mother's hand clutched tightly in mine. When the call came through a few days ago that she was ill, my sisters and I wasted no time packing our suitcases to come back to California. My mama had been there for us all of our lives. She raised us to be the strong, independent women we were today, fully supporting each of our decisions to move to New York, one by one, after graduating from high school. She encouraged us to see what else was out there, challenged us to figure out what we wanted to do with our lives, and chase those dreams... not that I had personally done much in the dream chasing department. But that was just because I didn't have any big aspirations yet. I'd conquered what I'd set out to do so far and had high hopes that someday I would figure out what I really wanted for my future.

There were eight of us sisters, and the only one who didn't move all the way across the United States was the youngest, Luna. After she graduated, she chose to stay in San Diego with our mother. Part of me wished I'd done the same, but my life was in New York now. I had a decent but somewhat boring job, several friends I spent Friday and Saturday nights with hanging out at clubs and listening to various bands who were hoping to climb their way to the top, and six of my sisters, who I loved dearly, living with me. I was happy, for the most part.

Sighing, I lowered my forehead to rest it against our clasped hands. Yes, I had a life in New York, but I missed my mom and Luna so much. I didn't necessarily miss sharing a room with two of my sisters in the house I grew up in, or the feeling of never having any privacy in our small home, but I could deal with that for now. I had more important things to worry about, like Mom's failing health, and helping out with her cleaning business, so she didn't lose her company while she was unable to run it. I would do whatever needed to be done to help, because that's what family did for one another.

"Everything is going to be okay, sweet Gabby."

My mother's voice was thin and raspy, but full of love. My heart thumped in my chest as I slowly raised my head to look into her compassionate eyes, my own shimmering with tears I was struggling to hold back. I was supposed to be the strong one in this situation, but it felt as if I was going to fall apart at any moment. Mom was our rock, the person who held our entire family together. I loved her so much, and seeing her lying helplessly in a hospital bed, looking so pale and weak, had my heart breaking.

"Mama, I..."

I didn't know how to continue. What do you say to the person who means more to you than anything else in the world, when you are terrified that they may not make it through the next few months? I blinked rapidly, refusing to let my tears fall.

"Hush now, sweetheart," Mama whispered, lifting a hand to gently cradle my cheek. "This is just another path I need to follow in this journey of life I'm on. It will all work out the way it is supposed to in the end."

I swallowed hard, nodding slowly as I reached up to swipe at the tears that had escaped, no matter how hard I fought to keep them hidden. "Yes, Mama."

"You have always been so vibrant, Gabriella. So full of joy." My mother's eyelids fluttered closed, her hand falling back to rest on the stark white sheet that covered her. "I am proud of you, my daughter."

"Thank you," I whispered, tears now streaming unchecked down my cheeks. "I love you so much, Mama."

"Love you too, baby," she murmured, before letting out a soft sigh and drifting off to sleep.

"Don't worry, we are going to take care of everything, Mama," I promised, leaning forward and placing a gentle kiss on her cheek. "You just rest."

CHAPTER 1

Gabriella

AFTER LETTING myself through the front door of Jameson Hughes' gorgeous mansion, worth over two million dollars, which I knew for a fact because I looked it up a couple of nights ago, I shut the door quietly behind me and leaned against it, my eyes slowly skating around the huge foyer.

It wasn't the first time I'd been there. I'd been taking care of his home and his recording studio, Wicked Chords Records, for the past three weeks. My mother owned a cleaning company called Reyes Cleaning Services, and my sisters, Catalina and Margo, were in charge of going over the client lists and handing out assignments after we arrived in California when it became apparent we were all going to be staying for a while. They gave me this one, knowing how much I loved music, and also that my favorite band, Rebellious Dynasty, was under contract with Jameson's company.

I was thrilled when they gave us our assignments and I found out I was heading to Wicked Chords. Luna, my youngest sister, had rolled her eyes, laughing at me when I let out a small squeal of excitement, but I didn't care. I couldn't wait to see what the inside of a real recording studio looked like.

I was not disappointed. It was one of the most amazing places

I'd ever seen. I always made sure to go in the middle of the night to clean when no one was there. That way, I could spend hours looking over the awards that decorated the walls throughout the building when I was finished. There were so many of them, I was in awe.

Jameson Hughes had built an empire, and I was more than impressed. Not only with his empire, but with the man himself. He captivated me like no one else ever had before, and it'd been that way since I saw my first image of him, when I was eighteen years old and it went public that he'd discovered Rebellious Dynasty. While all my friends were mooning over the rock stars he'd just signed to his recording label, I was enamored with Jameson and his piercing, dark eyes. Hot, panty-melting eyes that I couldn't get out of my head even now, years later.

Sighing, I pushed away from the door, knowing I needed to get started. Slipping off my shoes, I left them on the light brown mat in the entryway, then removed my sweatshirt and draped it over the banister that led upstairs, before heading toward the kitchen where I planned on starting my night. Normally, I would have already been in and out of the home before evening hours, but I was struggling with working full time and fulfilling my obligation to Reyes Cleaning Services with my sisters.

While I was grateful that I was able to keep the job I had in New York, as it was an online data entry position that I could do from home, if I could afford to, I would have quit a long time ago. It was tedious, boring, and held no appeal, but it was a job. I made my own schedule; the money was decent, and I had bills to pay. It wasn't my dream job, but then again, I didn't really have one of those. I wasn't sure what I wanted to do with my life. I'd gone to college, and had a diploma and business degree to prove it, but it wasn't necessarily a field I was interested in. It was a degree to help find a job, nothing more.

I hated coming so late to Jameson's home, but I knew he was out of town for a few days from a note I'd happened to see on his desk the last time I cleaned at Wicked Chords, so I figured it was safe enough to get done what needed to be done and get out of there without running into him. The place was huge, but it always appeared as if someone had already been there to clean before me. I wondered if Jameson was a neat freak, or if it was because he was never there? As beautiful as it was, the place seemed... empty. Lonely, even.

Sometimes I wondered if its owner felt the same way.

Shaking my head at my crazy thoughts, I slipped my earbuds into my ears, turned some music on, and got busy. The place wasn't going to clean itself, and my bed was calling my name.

CHAPTER 2

Jameson

I WAS SO TIRED. Utterly fucking exhausted. I'd just gotten back from a quick two-day trip to New York City, where I met with a promising, young, new music artist. Great voice, strong vocals, but unfortunately his online presence had me worried before I even boarded the plane that first day. I wish I would have followed my instincts and not wasted my time. The guy was an ass, plain and simple, and it hadn't taken me long after meeting him in person to realize I didn't want a prick like him associated with my music brand. I didn't care how far he was likely to go in his career, I'd spent many years making my recording company a business I could be proud of, I wasn't going to screw that up for anyone, least of all a spoiled, punk kid who thought the sun rose and set on him.

Coming to a stop in front of the black wrought-iron fence that surrounded my property, I lowered my window and keyed in the code that would open the gate. Scrubbing a hand over my face, I watched impatiently for it to open so I could drive through, not waiting for it to close before I drove down the paved driveway to my house. That's all it was, a house. I couldn't call it a home. I'd grown up in a home surrounded by family and love. This place was not that. I'd bought it three years ago because it went with the image I wanted to portray with the company I was building. Now, I found I was beyond worrying about that image. I just wanted a real home.

I frowned when I saw the lights on in the house, and then spotted the red, newer looking four-door car sitting in front of my garage. It was late, almost midnight, and whoever was there would have had to have the code to the gate to get in. That narrowed it down to my mother, one of my brothers, the lawn company, or the cleaning service I used. I had no idea what the hell any of them would be doing at my house so late. I didn't recognize the car, but that didn't mean anything. Someone in my family was always switching out cars. It could have been anyone.

Cursing under my breath, I hit the button to open the garage, then drove in. Whoever it was, they were leaving right fucking now.

It didn't take me long to get my briefcase and suitcase out of the trunk, and then I was heading into the mansion through a side door in the garage. It led into the kitchen, and I left my bags there while I went to find the person who was invading my space at this hour of the night.

The main floor was quiet, and I could smell the pleasant odor of the freshly cleaned area. I let my gaze wander around the large, spotless living room before walking into the foyer. A pair of small, white tennis shoes with a hot pink logo on the side sat near the door.

It was definitely not one of my brothers. And, while my mother would wear shoes similar to those, they would be in a much larger size. Which made me wonder what tiny, delicate feet fit in the ones I was staring at.

With my brow furrowing, I turned toward the stairs that went up to the second level of my house. By the scents that filled the air, it had to be someone from Reyes Cleaning Services, but I couldn't understand why they would be here so late. It didn't make sense. I honestly had no idea what time they normally showed up, but the place was always spotless when I came home from work, so I assumed it was during the day. They did a superb job, both at my house and at Wicked Chords, but I realized it had been weeks since I'd seen anyone at the studio. Normally, a woman arrived after hours and cleaned while I worked in my office. She was always there when I left, but we never talked. Lately, the building was still cleaned regularly, but Reyes Cleaning had to be taking care of it in the middle of the night.

Shoving a hand through my hair, I closed my eyes for a moment. Why hadn't I noticed it? I should have spotted a change like that immediately. Not that it mattered. They could work whatever hours they liked, as long as the job was done. I felt the same about my house, but right now, I was exhausted and just wanted to get some sleep before I had to be at the office for my early morning meeting.

With that thought in mind, I quickly scaled the stairs and then stalked down the hall, glancing in rooms as I passed by them. All lights were off except for the one in my bedroom, which was all the way at the end on the right-hand side. I paused for a moment before walking through the door, then froze when the sound of a female's low, sexy voice reached me. The song she was singing was an older one. One I knew, but I didn't focus on the lyrics so much as the sensual tone that seemed to flow through me, wrapping around me in a way that had my cock thickening for the first time in months in the jeans I wore.

"Jesus," I muttered, readjusting myself, biting back a groan as a shudder of pleasure ran through me.

It had been over a year since I'd last been with a woman. Unfortunately, I found out quickly after making my first million that most of them were more interested in my money and my status than me as a person. At first, it didn't bother me. I had my business to concentrate on and didn't want to get involved with anyone beyond the occasional one-night stand.

Eventually, when I decided maybe it was time to change that

one-night fling into something more, I got tired of trying to find someone who wanted me for *me* and finally just gave up. It took two bad relationships, each lasting less than a month, for me to come to the conclusion that I was better off alone. My mother didn't agree, but she wasn't the one wading through all the piranhas trying to find the right woman. It took a while, but she finally let it go, too.

Shaking my head, I pushed the thoughts aside and quickly crossed the room to look into my bathroom, coming to a hard stop in the doorway.

"Fuck," I rasped, my eyes immediately glued to the perfectly round bottom leaning over my large, jetted bathtub, wiggling back and forth to the music the woman was listening to. She had on a pair of denim booty shorts that the bottom swell of her ass cheeks peeked out of. She was on her knees, no socks, and I could see that her toes were painted a hot pink that matched the logo on her shoes downstairs. Dark brown hair with caramel highlights flowed down her back in a ponytail as she raised her head and belted out some high notes in the song.

I couldn't tear my gaze away from her, and a slow grin curved up the corners of my mouth as I crossed my arms, leaned against the doorjamb, and took in the show. I had no idea who she was, but I was going to find out.

Suddenly, the woman sat up and leaned back, her butt on her calves, as she removed her earbuds, slipped them into a pocket, and slid a phone from her shorts, tapping the front of it and setting it on the edge of the tub. Then she leaned back over it, those damn ass cheeks showing again, making me wonder if her skin was as soft there as it looked.

"Hey, Sissy!" she called out, still having no idea I was standing behind her. Feeling slightly guilty, I thought about saying something, but decided to wait for a few minutes.

"Gabby, where are you?"

"Well, right now I'm taking a dip in a swanky tub."

"Gabby…"

Gabby laughed, a loud, beautiful, carefree laugh that made me want to laugh with her. "I'm at Jameson's house."

Jameson? She called me by my first name, as if we already knew each other, and I found that I liked it. My name on her lips had my cock hardening even more, if that were possible. I wanted to hear it again, but in a much breathier tone as my hands skimmed over all that tantalizing, silky skin.

"His house? What are you doing there now? I thought you cleaned his house while he was at work and then cleaned his studio at night?"

"Normally, I do," Gabby said, sitting back again and rubbing the back of her wrist over her forehead. "He's out of town right now, though, so I didn't think he would mind if I waited until tonight."

Hell no, I didn't mind. Finding this woman in my bathroom, my cock coming alive after all this time, was the best thing that happened to me in a long time. The attraction was something I was definitely going to be exploring, as long as beautiful Gabby was willing.

"How do you know he's out of town?"

I was wondering the same thing, but found I didn't want to interrupt the byplay between the two women to ask my own questions.

"I saw a note on his desk when I was there last night."

"Gabby! You went through his things? You know Mom doesn't allow that!"

"No, Luna, I did not go through his things," Gabby responded in a sassy tone that had me biting back laughter. "However, I do clean his office. It was sitting there on his desk, in plain sight. I couldn't help but read it."

I knew which note she was talking about now. I'd written it myself, on a piece of paper that I put beside my calendar instead of actually putting it on the calendar itself. It was a reminder to get my little nephew, Theodore, a birthday present when I got back in town on Saturday. Today was Friday, which meant I was back a day earlier than planned. No wonder she thought she was safe.

"Well, when do you think you will be home?" came her sister's soft reply.

"Why? You already back from your date with your sexy daddy?" Gabby teased, as she grabbed a hold of the side of the tub and pushed herself to her feet.

"Oh god," Luna groaned loudly, "I never should have told you about that, Gabriella Reyes!"

Sexy daddy? This conversation was getting more and more interesting, and I was starting to feel guilty for letting it go on so long without letting them know they weren't alone.

"Ah, Luna, don't be angry," Gabby said with laughter in her voice as she leaned down to grab her phone, the rag she'd been using to wipe down the bathtub in her other hand. "If I had a man who looked like that and wanted to give me multiple orgasms, and his only requirement was that I call him daddy, I would do it in a heartbeat."

"Really?" Luna asked so softly, I almost didn't catch it.

Gabby turned toward me and froze, her pretty brown eyes widening in horror as her gaze met mine. Her tongue slipped out to wet her full, luscious pink lips, her cheeks flaming a bright red.

It was obvious she was embarrassed, but I stayed where I was, leaning casually against the doorjamb, even though I felt anything but casual as I waited for her reply. Not because I was into the whole daddy thing, but because I wanted to see if she would be honest with me standing there watching her.

Damn, just a few minutes ago I was ready to kick whoever was in my house out so I could get some sleep. Now, while I was still exhausted, I was feeling the first stirrings of excitement I'd felt in a long time. She wasn't just beautiful; the woman was breathtaking.

"Gabby?" Luna said, her voice wavering with nerves. "Would you really call him daddy?"

MY MOUTH DROPPED open in complete shock, as I stared at the gorgeous man who stood in front of me dripping with sexy authority. I wanted to find a hole to hide in, one I'd live in for the rest of my life. Not only was I in his house in the middle of the night without his knowledge, but I was wearing my shortest pair of shorts and a tight, light pink, spaghetti strap tank top. Definitely not something my mother would approve of when cleaning one of her elite client's houses.

"Gabby?"

I stiffened at the small hint of fear that had crept into my sister's voice, hating that I was the reason it was there. Luna was the baby of the family, and the one I was closest to. She was my best friend, and that never changed just because I moved so far away.

Determined to set her mind at ease, I straightened my shoulders, lifted my chin defiantly, and said, "You better believe it, Sissy. If I found a man like your Oliver, one who wanted to love and cherish me, spoil me the way he does you, I would call him whatever the hell he wanted."

Luna giggled, then whispered, "He doesn't love me, but thank you, Gabs."

"He would be stupid not to," I said, meaning it. There was no better person out there than my baby sister. "Now, I need to finish up here, but I will be home soon, okay? Give me half an hour?"

"Okay. Be safe."

"Always."

Taking a deep breath, I disconnected the call and shoved the phone in my back pocket. I needed to tread lightly. Jameson Hughes was one of mom's highest paying clients. She would not be happy with me if I lost his business because of my big mouth.

"I apologize, Mr. Hughes," I said, clutching the damp cloth I still held tightly. "I was just finishing up, and I will be out of your way soon."

Tilting his head to the side, his dark eyes dancing with mirth, he said, "I think I liked it better when you called me Jameson."

I closed my eyes, swallowing hard. He'd heard my entire conversation, it would seem. Great, just great. That meant he knew I'd snooped through his desk, too.

"Tell me, Gabriella," he said, his lips curved up into a small, devilish grin, his eyes lit with curiosity, "are you into the Daddy-Dom thing like your sister?"

I felt my face flush even more, and knew it had to be a deep, dark red now. Oh. My. God. I was not having this conversation with Jameson fucking Hughes. Turning, I walked over to a small pile of towels and picked them up, holding them to my chest as I went to move past him. "I will just take these dirty towels and put them in the washer before I leave, Mr. Hughes."

I hesitated a moment. Crap, I should dry them too.

Jameson's hand shot out, and he rested it on my hip before I could try to sneak past him. He placed his knuckle under my chin and gently raised my head until our eyes met. "It's late. Leave the towels on the washer and I will take care of them." When I would have protested, he shook his head. "Leave them, Gabriella. I'm running on eight hours of sleep in the past two days, and I can tell you are tired too. Go home, get some rest. Leave the towels."

My heart was racing. A part of me was mortified and wanted to run. Another part—a part that had waited years to meet the man who was so close to me now, didn't want to move a muscle. "My mama wouldn't like that."

His eyes narrowed on me. "Gabriella Reyes. Your mother must own Reyes Cleaning Services?"

"Yes," I whispered, biting my bottom lip, worrying it with my teeth. What did I do now? I had really screwed up tonight. I never should have come to a client's house so late. I should have worn appropriate attire, no matter what time I came. I should not have had a very inappropriate conversation with my baby sister on speaker phone in the man's bathroom. And last, I shouldn't walk out without the job completed... but I knew that was exactly what I was about to do.

As I watched, Jameson's gaze went to my lips, then slowly trailed lower to rest on my breasts. I groaned silently when I realized what he was looking at. The towels I was holding onto were now sitting right below my breasts, pushing them up and putting my nipples on display. They'd always been sensitive and with being this close to the object of my obsession for the past several years, they were hard and pressing against my tank. It didn't help that I wasn't wearing a bra.

Jameson pushed away from the side of the door and took a step closer to me, holding me still with the hand that was on my hip, his other hand moving to cup my cheek. When his head began to lower slowly, I should have stepped back. I should have tried to stop him. Should have done something. Anything.

I didn't.

Instead, I just waited, confused as hell about what was happening, but unwilling to stop it.

His mouth touched mine lightly, just a soft brushing, his tongue sliding over my bottom lip, before he raised his head again.

17

His hand slid around to cradle the back of my neck as he ground out, "You taste so fucking good, baby. Just as good as I thought you would."

A shudder ran through me at the lust in his gaze, eyes so dark now they were almost black. My pussy clenched and then began to pulse at his rough tone, my body going taut with desire. I wanted him to do more than just kiss me. I wanted to feel those hands he was holding me close with, moving all over my body. I wanted to drop the towels I was clutching so tightly and move into him, taking what I needed.

I'd never felt like this before. I had sex a total of two times in my life. They both sucked. The only orgasms I'd ever received were ones I'd given myself. The way my entire body was on fire right now, I was positive that wouldn't be the case with Jameson Hughes.

The problem was, I didn't know him. Not really. Only what I'd seen in magazines and on social media over the past six years. Not only that, but he didn't know me. At all. If this went any further, it would be nothing more than a night of meaningless sex for him. It would mean so much more to me. Which was stupid, because once again, I didn't know the man.

I couldn't do it. No matter how much I wanted to, I just couldn't.

"I have to go," I whispered, slowly stepping back from him.

"Hold on a second." My eyes widened when he reached around me and slipped my phone from my back pocket. As I watched, he pulled up my contacts, put in his name and number, then returned it to my pocket. "I'd like to see you again, Gabriella, but the ball's in your court. Call me, or text me if it makes you feel more comfortable."

"Why?" I asked in confusion. Why did he want to see me? He was everything I wasn't. Successful, rich, famous. Hell, I worked a data entry job that was so damn boring I could do it in my sleep. I

18

cleaned his house. We just met, not ten minutes ago. What could he possibly see in me?

"Because," he said huskily. "Everything I've seen about you so far intrigues me, Gabriella Reyes, and I want to get to know you."

His mouth met mine again, and I whimpered softly. I couldn't believe this was happening to me. Jameson Hughes, hotshot music producer and owner of Wicked Chords Records, was kissing me. He wanted me to call him—wanted to see me again.

Jameson groaned, the grip on my neck tightening as he deepened the kiss, his tongue sliding between my lips, slipping into my mouth. I moaned, unable to stop the sound from emerging. His tongue found mine, and he tangled them together in an erotic dance, making me drop the towels to the floor. My hands went to his chest, sliding over the black T-shirt that covered it, curving into fists to grasp it tightly.

Pulling back, Jameson rested his forehead against mine, closing his eyes. "You better get going, Gabriella, or I won't let you go, and we both know you aren't ready for something like that."

"Jameson." I breathed his name, unsure of what I wanted to say, as I stood there trembling with hot, fiery desire racing through me.

The hand on my hip pulled me closer until I felt the hard length of his erection pressing against my belly. Jameson let out a deep groan, lowering his head to my neck and kissing it gently just once before he pulled back. "Come on, baby. I'll walk you out."

My eyes met his, another small whimper slipping out. Holy shit. What was I doing? What the hell was happening?

Not saying a word, I squeezed past him and walked quickly out of his room, down the hall, and then ran lightly down the stairs. Grabbing my sweatshirt off the banister, I slid it on to cover my obviously aroused state. I was shoving my feet into my shoes when I heard Jameson coming down the stairs toward me.

I didn't know what to do. I was embarrassed as hell and unsure of what to do next. I had to get out of there.

I grasped the doorknob, but then stopped, turning back to look at Jameson. He stood just a few feet away, his eyes locked on me. I had no idea what to say, so I faced the door again and opened it, no part of me wanting to walk through it.

"Gabriella."

I glanced back, my gaze meeting his, but stayed silent.

"I have a meeting in the morning, followed by two others throughout the day, but would love to see you tomorrow night."

I still didn't get it. The man could have anyone he wanted. I was sure women were lined up waiting for the chance to date him. Why would he waste his time with someone like me? What about me could be so intriguing that he would even want to?

"Dinner?" He named one of the nicest restaurants in San Diego, but I shook my head.

When his eyes darkened over in what I thought was disappointment, I admitted softly, "I don't think I would be comfortable in a place like that. I wouldn't want to embarrass you."

Jameson frowned but didn't argue. "Then dinner here. Six o'clock?"

I didn't agree, but I didn't turn him down, either. I needed time to think—to figure out what the hell was going on.

"I'll text you," I finally said, before turning to leave. I wasn't committing to anything just yet.

"Drive safe, sweet Gabby," were the last words I heard before the door shut behind me.

CHAPTER 4

Jameson

I'm an idiot, I thought for what had to be the hundredth time as I sat in my third meeting of the day on Saturday. This was the last one, thank fuck. I'd set them all up myself, but was regretting it, as were my employees. I could tell they were all ready to go home to their families. I wanted to leave too, but I was beating myself up, because while I'd programmed my number into Gabriella's phone, I hadn't gotten hers. I did it on purpose at the time because I knew I was coming on strong and was starting to scare her off. I'd wanted to give her the chance to contact me, but it was late afternoon now, and I was regretting it.

My account manager was going over something with the books when my phone vibrated. I glanced at it and was unaware when the wide grin spread across my face.

It's Gabby.

That was all it said. I could see the little bubbles appearing and leaving, like she was typing more, but was unsure of what to say. After quickly programming her name and number into my phone, I answered.

Hey, baby. I'm almost finished for the day. I hope you like steak.

The bubbles I'd been watching stopped. I glanced back up at the presentation Dani was giving as I waited impatiently for Gabriella to reply. I glanced down when my phone went off again.

Gabby: What can I bring?

My thoughts went wild with ideas, all things I would never say to her right now when she was so skittish about what was happening between us.

Just yourself.

Gabby: Did you get Theodore a present?

I swore softly when I realized I hadn't, and his birthday party was tomorrow at noon.

Thank you for reminding me. I'll grab something on the way home. I glanced at my watch and sighed. **Seven instead, okay?**

Those bubbles started again, then stopped, then started. Then I read:

Gabby: What does he like? I'm out with Luna now. I could grab him something for you?

I was aware that Dani was winding up her speech in the background, but my gaze was stuck on the last text from Gabby. She was offering to get my nephew a birthday present from me? I didn't know what to think about that. I'd never had a woman pick up a present for one of my nieces or nephews before. Hell, I'd never had a woman I even talked to about my family before.

Gabby: Seven is okay. See you then.

My grip tightened on my phone. I'd waited too long to reply. Somehow, I knew I'd made her nervous about volunteering to help, and I didn't like that.

He will be five. Loves everything to do with action figures. Spider Man is his favorite. See you at six, baby.

Gabby: See you then.

I found I couldn't just leave it at that. I didn't want her worried about anything. I wanted her to have fun shopping with her sister. I wanted her to be happy. Wanted things I had no right wanting after just meeting the woman.

One more thing.

Gabby: Yes?

You never did tell me. Are you into the Daddy-Dom thing?

Those little bubbles went crazy, then I saw,

Gabby: Guess you will have to find out.

I let out a burst of laughter that I didn't bother trying to hold back. I had a feeling the woman was about to take me on a wild ride, one I welcomed.

I look forward to it, beautiful.

Shoving back my chair, I shot a grin at my employees. "Sorry, I need to get going. Have a great rest of your weekend, and I will see you on Monday."

"But, Mr. Hughes, we haven't discussed everything on your list," my assistant, Henry, sputtered out in confusion. "There are still a few items you wanted to address."

"Those items will be there for the next meeting," I said, making my way to the door. "I've taken up enough of your time on a Saturday."

I left the room, heading to my office to finish up a couple of things, so I could get home and start dinner. I was ready to explore where this thing with Gabriella might lead.

CHAPTER 5

Gabriella

I stood on Jameson's front step, tapping my heel anxiously as I waited for him to answer the door. I'd changed my outfit six times, finally settling on the very first one I had put on, and I was already regretting it. I decided on a white sundress covered in bright yellow daisies, with a short matching yellow sweater and yellow sandals. It was both sweet and sexy at the same time. I should have gone with jeans and a long sleeve top, maybe paired with my short boots.

The door opened, and it was too late to run back home and change. Jameson stood there in a pair of faded blue jeans and a burgundy-colored shirt that hugged his body. His hair was dark and thick and full on top, shorter on the sides, his beard trimmed short. His feet were bare. This was a side of him that no one else saw. At least, not when the press was around. He was always dressed in a suit and tie, with polished dress shoes. The man was sexy as sin either way, and just the sight of him made my pulse begin to race and my mouth go dry.

"I brought gifts," I said, raising the three large bags I was holding. "Hopefully, Theodore likes them. If not, I have the receipts and you can take them back. Or maybe he already has them. I don't know. I got several things, just in case."

I was rambling, but I couldn't help it. I'd never shopped for a little boy before and was praying I did okay. If not, hopefully Jameson had time to exchange them before the party. I realized that I didn't even know when that was.

Reaching out, he took one of the bags from my hand, and held the door open wider so I could come in. "I'm sure whatever you got is great. I really appreciate you doing this, Gabriella. The party's tomorrow at noon, and if you hadn't said something, I would have forgotten all about it."

I smiled, shaking my head. "No, you wouldn't have. He's family. Besides..." I shrugged, winking at him. "You had a note to remind you."

Jameson threw back his head and laughed as he shut the door and then led the way into the kitchen. "Yes, you're correct, and I looked right over that note all day while I was at work." There was a massive island in the middle of the kitchen that he set the bag down on before turning and walking toward the door that led out to the back patio. "Let me flip the steaks, and then you can show me what you bought."

Climbing up onto one of the bar stools in front of the island, I set my bags down next to the other one, and then slowly started pulling out some of the things I bought. When Jameson walked back in, his eyebrows rose.

I shrugged, giving him a small smile. "I wasn't sure what to buy, so I thought you could choose from them."

Without a word, he crossed the room and came to a stop right in front of me. Cupping my cheeks in his hands, he lowered his head and captured my mouth with his. I gasped in surprise, and his tongue slipped inside. It was a slow, deep kiss, one that had me panting softly when he finally pulled back.

"Thank you, Gabriella," he said gruffly. "You don't know what this means to me."

Biting my lip, I lowered my eyes to his chest, feeling my cheeks flush. "I'm glad I could help." And I was. That was me. I loved to do what I could for everyone. It made my heart happy to make them happy.

"Let's see what you got."

I nodded, reaching for the first bag. Jameson moved, so he was standing just behind me, his hand resting on the counter next to me as he looked over my shoulder. It put his front up close to my back, and a part of me wanted to lean back against him and feel that solid chest against me.

"You said he is going to be five, so I assume he has a twin-sized bed?" I pulled out the sheets and pillowcase I bought, followed by a comforter. "Spidey is on here, but so are a lot of the other superheroes, so I thought he might like that." Picking up the pillow I'd already set out, I put it beside the comforter. "Since Spidey is his favorite, I got him a special pillow just with him on it. And then I saw this awesome stuffed figure to go with it." I paused, "I'm not sure if he likes that sort of thing, but I thought you might know."

"Yeah, he does," Jameson said, running a hand through the hair that flowed over my shoulders and down my back. I'd left it down on purpose today, hoping he would like it. "He has one that he takes everywhere with him, but my sister-in-law is always saying he needs a new one because his is falling apart. This one is different from the one he has now. I bet he will love it."

I smiled, gaining more confidence as I gestured to some other things I'd laid out on the island. "At his age, he should be brushing his teeth daily, so I got him a toothbrush, toothpaste, and then I couldn't pass up the bubble bath."

"All with his favorite heroes on it," Jameson muttered. "He is going to love them, and so will Jenni, because these things are good for him."

"Who's Jenni?" I asked, looking over my shoulder at him, catching my breath at how close he was.

"My sister-in-law," he said, his eyes going to my lips before coming back to meet mine.

"That's right. You have two brothers."

27

"How did you know that?" he asked, his eyes narrowing on me.

"Social media, Jameson. Most of your life isn't exactly a secret."

For some reason, he didn't seem happy with my reply, but all he said was, "Yeah, I have two brothers, Toby and Chandler. Toby is married to Jenni, and they have two children. Theodore, who you know will be five tomorrow, and Alyssa just turned eight. Chandler's wife is Maryanne, and they have triplets. Sarah, Skylar, and Stephen are ten."

"Oh, wow," I whispered. "Triplets."

"Maryanne loves it," Jameson said with a wide smile. "She says they were only planning on having two children. She has three now, so they are done. She doesn't have to go through any of it again."

I giggled, shaking my head. "I don't blame her." Without thinking, I leaned up and placed a kiss on his jaw before turning back to the presents now covering the island. I missed the small catch in his breath as I started pointing out more things. "Okay, so I also bought him this puzzle with action heroes on it, so you are giving him something somewhat educational, even though it is basically a toy and fun. It's teaching him to match up the pieces, so I figured it would work. A book, because he's probably around that age where they are learning to read, and then a couple of action figures, because if you are going for favorite uncle, you have to put actual toys in there somewhere."

I felt his arms go around me from behind and pull me close, up against that hard chest I was just dreaming about leaning on. "It all sounds perfect, Gabriella."

My heart began to flutter at the tone of his voice, and I leaned back to look up at him. "I'm glad. I also got wrapping paper, bows, and a card." When his gaze went to the presents and his brow creased in the adorable frown he always gave, I laughed. "I figured I could wrap them for you before I left, if you are okay with all of them."

"Thank fuck," he growled, lowering his head to bury it in my neck. Nibbling lightly on my skin there, he admitted, "I have no idea how to wrap them. I always buy the gifts myself, but I take them to my mom to wrap before the party."

Tilting my head to the side to give him more access as he trailed his tongue over my shoulder and up the sensitive skin on my neck, I murmured, "Don't worry, I have you covered this time."

He bit down gently on my earlobe, then sucked it into his mouth before muttering, "Thanks, baby."

I loved the way he called me that. Baby. As if I was someone special to him. I knew it wasn't true. While I believed in love and happily ever after, I wasn't sure Jameson Hughes did. I'd never once seen him in a committed relationship on any of the social media outlets, nor in the news. There were times he attended music award ceremonies and other banquets with a stunning woman on his arm, but it never went further than that, as far as I could tell. My guess was he kept that part of his life away from the media's attention, but that he did casual relationships. Nothing lasting. Which is what he would be offering me. A few days, maybe a couple of weeks, of fun. That was it.

No matter how much I might want it to be more, I wasn't going to bet my heart on it.

CHAPTER 6

Jameson

SHE FOLLOWED me on social media. It made sense. As sexy and beautiful as her voice was, she probably followed a lot of singers and bands, along with their producers. Maybe she had dreams of a record deal herself, which, by the sounds of her voice the night before, I could easily make happen.

But I didn't want that to be the reason she was sitting across my dining room table eating dinner with me right now. I didn't want her to be out buying my nephew presents just so she could get a shot with me to further a singing career, or for anything to do with my company or money. I wanted her to like me for me, which had me double thinking everything right now. Dredging up dark, hurtful memories I would rather forget. I didn't want her to be like every other woman I tried to bring into my life. I wanted her to be different.

"Tell me a little bit about yourself," I said, trying to shove those memories and doubts away so I could enjoy the evening. "From what I heard last night; I take it you live with your sister?"

Gabriella's face clouded over, and I was surprised to see a hint of sadness appear. "Actually, I live in New York."

"New York?" That surprised me. If she lived in New York, what was she doing cleaning for me?

"I have eight sisters," she said quietly. "We grew up here, raised by our mother. My father passed away when Luna was two. She's the youngest. We all moved away to New York when we graduated from high school. Mama wanted us to get away and see what life had to offer. Only Luna stayed."

"All of you moved to the same city?"

A soft smile appeared, and Gabriella nodded. "Yes, we share a place out there. We all have jobs. I work for a company doing data entry, which means I am able to still do that now while we are here."

"So, not only do you work full time, but you clean my house and my office at Wicked Chords?" I wasn't sure what to think of that. It meant she was a hard worker, which I liked, but she deserved to enjoy life too.

"Yes, for now. Luna called a few weeks ago to let us know Mama was in the hospital," Gabriella whispered, lowering her head to look at her food. "She has cancer. So, we all moved back to help with her company."

"I'm so sorry, baby." I hated the sorrow I saw in her eyes when she lifted her gaze to mine. Reaching over, I placed a hand on hers. "She's tough, Gabriella. She has to be to run a company the way she does. She will pull through this."

Gabriella nodded, turning her hand over and grasping mine. "Yes, she is. She's a fighter. She's fought all her life for us, and now we will fight for her. She's the reason we are all home again."

"Whatever the reason, I'm glad you're here."

The corners of her mouth tipped up into a small smile. "Me too."

"So, tell me about your dreams," I said, trying to put a smile back on her face. "Are you going to college? Do you know what you want to do in the future? I don't get the impression you love your job right now." If she had, she would have mentioned more about it besides the fact that she still had it.

Tugging her hand from mine, she went back to her food, taking a bite of steak and eating it slowly before she answered. "Honestly, I'm not sure what I want to do. I actually have a college degree, a business one, but I have no idea what I want to do with it. I took the job I have now with the idea of moving up in the company, but..."

"But what?" I asked, curious as to where she was going with it.

Gabriella sighed, placing her fork on her plate, and sitting back in her chair. "It's boring. My job is so boring, and I don't think moving positions within the company is going to help. I've looked into some that have come available in the past couple of years and have had no desire to apply for them."

"So, it sounds to me like what you need to do is find a different career entirely," I said, watching her closely. "There are a lot of things you can do with a business degree."

"True. I just have to figure out what I want, but it is going to have to wait. Right now, Mom comes first."

Gabriella rose and took her plate into the kitchen. I could hear her cleaning up as I quickly finished my dinner and then went in to help her. No matter how hard I tried, there was no way to twist around anything she was saying, to make me think she was after me to further a singing career or wanted money. She was open and honest about every question I asked.

I found her leaning over the dishwasher, the hem of her little dress rising up so far, that once again I was blessed with the small curve of her ass cheek. This time, I didn't hesitate. Setting my dishes on the counter beside her, I moved in close and placed my palms on the backs of her legs, slowly sliding them up until they cradled that skin that had been taunting me yesterday and was doing it again today.

"Jameson," she whispered, and I felt the tremble that ran through her.

"You are so fucking beautiful, Gabriella," I rasped, sliding my hands up to her hips and pulling her against my straining erection. I found the soft skin of her neck again, that place I loved to tease with my tongue, and began to lick and nibble my way across her shoulder to the strap of her dress. She'd taken off the sweater before we sat down to eat, which meant I had access to even more of the soft skin. It wasn't enough.

"I need to touch you, baby. All of you."

"Yes," she breathed, leaning back against me, her arm coming up to curl around, so her fingers threaded through the back of my hair.

We'd been dancing this dance all night. My dick became hard the moment I set eyes on her after I opened the door, and hadn't gone down since. The ways she'd been giving me those covert, blushing glances of hers, I knew she was feeling the same way. She wanted me. I wanted her. And I was done waiting.

My hand moved over Gabriella's stomach and lower, under the waistband of her panties and inside. She moaned when I found her clit with one finger, teasing it for a moment before moving lower, sliding through her wet lips and inside her.

Fuck, I couldn't wait to feel her surrounding my length with all that soaking wet heat. I slipped another finger inside her, then began to rub her clit with my thumb.

"Oh god!" she moaned as the hand in my hair tightened, and she began moving her hips back and forth, while she fucked herself on my fingers. I slid my other hand up under the top of her dress, groaning when I found her bare breast waiting. I didn't think she was wearing a bra and just confirmed it. Her nipple was hard, and I pinched it lightly, loving the soft cries coming from Gabriella when I did. "Please. Oh god, Jameson!"

"Come for me, baby," I demanded, my thumb on her clit moving faster. "I want to feel it." I pinched her nipple harder than before, biting down softly on her shoulder, and Gabriella flew apart in my arms, screaming my name.

It was the sexiest fucking thing I'd ever been a part of.

"That was..."

I looked down into her deep brown eyes swirling darkly with desire, and replied, "Yeah, baby, it was." Wonderful, amazing, fan-fucking-tastic, and I wanted more. "Come upstairs with me. I need you in my bed, your taste on my tongue, and your pussy wrapped around my cock. I fucking need you."

Her eyes widened, her mouth opening slightly, and then she slowly nodded. "Yes, I want that. All of that."

Groaning, I slipped my hand from her panties, lifting my fingers to my mouth to lick her cream from them.

"Jameson," she gasped in shock, before a moan slipped out. I spun her around, lifting her up until her legs locked around my waist. "You sure about this, Gabriella?" I asked, giving her one last out.

In response, she covered my mouth with hers, for the first time taking control, and slid her tongue past my lips. Her arms went around my neck, and she clung to me as she kissed me. My cock was so hard, I almost took her right there on the kitchen floor, but she deserved better than that for our first time.

Our first time...

Because if I had my way, this would be the beginning of a future that included many more nights of Gabriella Reyes ending up in my bed.

CHAPTER 7

Gabriella

I WAS aware of Jameson carrying me up to his room, and then my back was against the soft, brown and blue comforter on his king-sized bed, my dress up around my waist. His eyes were taking in the small, white, lacey thong I wore, with the light pink heart in the center of a bow on the front.

He groaned my name, and then my brand-new panties, ones I'd bought just for him that day when I was out with Luna, were torn from my body. He licked his lips as he stared at my bare pussy. It was another stop my baby sister and I made today. It was actually the first place we went to, and where we got manicures, pedis, and waxed. I knew the moment I woke up this morning the way my night was going to end, so it didn't take much for Luna to talk me into a trip to the spa in the city. Normally, I did the waxing myself, but I always left a small strip of hair down the middle. But Luna talked me into a full-on Brazilian wax, going completely bare for the first time, and it looked like it had been a good decision. After the spa, of course, was the lingerie shop. Then the adult toy store, although that last one was my suggestion.

"I love you like this," Jameson growled, running his hands

down my legs, then back up to my thighs. "Your legs open, your pussy bare, glistening with your wet juices."

"Oh god, Jameson," I moaned, reaching for him. "I need you."

"Not yet, baby," he muttered, grasping my hips and pulling me down toward the end of the bed. "I want to taste you first. I want you to come on my tongue, and then again when I'm so deep inside you, you never forget who you belong to."

I froze, my heart pounding in my chest as I stared at him in shock. "Who I belong to?"

"Yes, Gabriella. You are mine. Mine to touch, to kiss, to lick, to bury myself inside. You belong to me, understand?"

Holy shit, Jameson Hughes was staking his claim on me. Gabriella Reyes. The question was, did I want him to? The answer was simple. Yes! I would belong to him for as long as he would have me.

"As long as you understand that it goes both ways, Jameson. If I'm yours, you are mine. This is mine," I said, reaching down to grasp his cock through his jeans. When he groaned and pushed into my touch, I said, "Mine, and only mine. I won't share."

"Me neither," he growled, his eyes locked on mine.

I nodded slowly, then let go of him to lie back against the bed. "Then yes, I belong to you."

I wasn't stupid. I knew it wouldn't be long term. There was no forever in our future. We would have our fun now, staying exclusive until he was ready to move on, and then I would move on too. Back to New York, and the boring, dismal life I lived out there. But, until then, I would have Jameson.

His eyes burning with possessiveness, he lowered his head until he hovered over my aching pussy. "This is mine," he muttered, as his tongue snaked out and licked right up my bare lips. He licked me again, and again, and then his tongue was inside me and he was eating his fill.

I cried out his name, tangling my fingers in his thick hair, arching up into his mouth. He licked and sucked, moving up to my clit and giving it attention, before going back to delve into my pussy. His tongue was fucking magic, and soon I was falling apart, screaming for him as I was thrown into my second orgasm that night.

I heard the sound of a zipper, then Jameson pulled me down so my hips hung just over the edge of the bed, and he lifted my legs up around his waist. "Look at me," he rasped, as I felt the head of his cock pushing against my entrance. "Baby, look at me when I take you. *See me.*"

The way he said it confused me for a moment. The need in not only his voice but also his gaze added to that confusion. I kept my eyes on his as he pushed slowly into me, so hard and thick, filling me completely. He paused once he was fully seated deep inside, leaning over my body, his arms resting on the bed beside me, his eyes still on mine.

I raised a hand and placed it on his jaw, my other hand going to grasp one of his. "I see you, Jameson," I whispered, still not fully understanding what he needed from me, but knowing it was important. "I see you."

He swallowed hard and then his jaw clenched as he covered my hand with his, lacing our fingers together as he began to move. He went slowly at first, thrusting deep and hard, driving me out of my mind. Then he had my arms over my head, holding both of my wrists tightly in one hand as he leaned down and pulled one of my nipples into his mouth, sucking hard. Grasping my hip, he began to pound harder and faster, his mouth leaving one breast to go to the other.

"Jameson, please, I'm so close," I moaned, unlocking my heels from his back and placing them on the bed. I arched up into him, meeting him thrust for thrust, needing something that was just out of my reach. It was building inside me, wild and crazy, just waiting to burst free, and it did when Jameson suddenly bit down on my nipple, sending a flash of pain through me, pushing me over the edge. I screamed as I came, my pussy clamping down tight on his cock, and then convulsing around it in the most powerful orgasm I'd ever had in my life.

"Fuck, baby, so tight," Jameson groaned, letting go of my wrists and rising up. Grasping my hips tightly, he held me still as he slammed into me again and again, until he stiffened, and then roared my name as he spilled inside of me. "Perfect," he muttered, leaning down to kiss my lips, holding me against him for a moment. "So fucking perfect."

"Agreed," I whispered, running my hand through his hair. He was perfect.

After one last kiss, he pulled out of me and gathered me in his arms. Sliding the covers back, he laid me on his bed and then went to the bathroom. He was back within minutes with a hand towel to help me clean up, then he used it and tossed it toward the hamper before crawling into bed beside me and pulling me close.

"Stay with me."

Laying against his shoulder, I trailed my hand through the hair on his chest. "For a while."

He was quiet for a moment, then said, "Tell me about Gabriella Reyes."

"What would you like to know?"

"Everything. From when you were born, to what you always wanted to be when you grew up, to the woman you are now."

I laughed softly, snuggling closer to him. "Well, I'm twenty-four years old. I already told you about my family. When I was younger, I wanted to be several things. A teacher, an astronaut, an actress, but mostly I loved to sing."

I felt Jameson stiffen beneath me. Then he let out a deep breath. "You want to be a singer?"

"No, not anymore. That was what teenage me wanted to be."

"What changed?" He seemed to hesitate before he said, "Because I've heard you sing, Gabby. If you wanted to follow that career, if it is a dream of yours, I could make it happen."

I yawned, shaking my head as I wrapped my arm around his

waist. "No, honey, I don't want to be a singer. I just do it for fun now. But thank you."

"You're sure?"

"Positive. I have no desire to sing in front of a bunch of people, Jameson." I yawned again, exhaustion setting in. "I'll save that for you and family."

It was strange, but suddenly it felt as if all the tension drained out of him, and then he held me tighter. "Sounds good to me, baby."

"I wouldn't turn down some Rebellious Dynasty tickets, though, as long as you went with me."

Jameson chuckled, his chest shaking under my cheek. "You like them, do you?"

"Love them," I admitted softly, closing my eyes as I felt sleep trying to claim me. "That's how I found you."

"What?"

"When you signed them so long ago, that was the first time I saw your face. I've been a Jameson Hughes groupie ever since," I teased, laughing softly. "It's your eyes."

"You like my eyes?"

"I love everything about you," I murmured, "but your eyes are my favorite. Dark, piercing, mysterious. I've dreamed of them so many times."

"Go to sleep, Gabriella," Jameson whispered, kissing me gently on the top of my head.

"Jameson?"

"Yeah, baby?"

"I like belonging to you."

"Good, I like it too."

CHAPTER 8

Jameson

WAKING up in an empty bed was not how I'd hoped my Sunday morning would start. She was gone. Beautiful, sweet, funny Gabby had left long enough ago that her side of the bed was cold.

Sighing, I looked at the clock and groaned when I saw it was almost eleven. That didn't give me much time to get ready and get over to my brother's house for the birthday party. After one last look at the empty side of my bed, I rose and went into the bathroom to take a quick shower.

Twenty minutes later, I was standing in front of the island in my kitchen, looking at all the presents for my nephew that my woman had wrapped and put back in the bags for me to take. I reached out and touched one of the bags, hardly able to believe that I had finally found someone who seemed to care about me and not about what I could do for them. After our conversation last night, one I was fairly certain Gabriella was half asleep for, all of my doubts were starting to disappear.

A goofy grin crossed my lips. She liked my eyes—had liked them for years.

Shaking my head at myself, I went to gather up the bags full of presents when I saw the note.

Jameson,

I hope Theodore enjoys his gifts and you get the award for favorite uncle! Sorry I have to leave, but I need to clean at Wicked Chords, so it's ready for you on Monday. I prefer working Saturday night rather than Sunday because I try to start my other job by seven in the morning. That, and I might be hoping to spend more time with you tomorrow night.

Have a wonderful day with your family!

Gabby

Shit. I'd forgotten about her cleaning at the office. I didn't like her working in the middle of the night, but she was doing it for her mother, and I refused to become the overbearing dickhead boyfriend who started telling her what to do all the time.

Boyfriend... was that what I was to her? Hell, I'd claimed her the night before, and she'd claimed me right back. I preferred the word man over boyfriend, though. Yeah, I was hers. Her man.

Grabbing my phone, I sent her a text.

Thanks for wrapping the presents, baby. Means a lot to me.

It did mean a lot. I would have wrapped them, but I had no idea how to. I'd never wrapped a present in my life. Although Christmas was coming up in a few months. Maybe Gabby would show me how. She'd done an amazing job on Theodore's. My phone vibrated, and I glanced at the message that came over.

Gabby: You're welcome! Have fun at the party. Don't eat too much cake!

I chuckled, shaking my head.

I don't like cake.

Gabby: What? You don't like cake? What's wrong with you?

Maybe I would like it better if I could lick it off you.

Gabby: We could try it. Bring some home. We'll experiment.

Fuck me. No, I didn't like cake, but I would eat a whole damn sheet of it if I got to lick it off my woman.

Gabby: You're going to be late.

I glanced at my watch. She was right. I needed to leave, but I wanted to sit there and talk to her. I just saw her the night before, but I already missed her smile, her laugh, and her lips. My dick started to get hard, and I quickly shot down that thought. I was about to go to a birthday party for a five-year-old with my family. I had no time to find any kind of relief first, and if I did, I would want it to be inside Gabriella, not with my hand.

As always, you are right, beautiful. I'm going now. Miss you.

I hesitated before pushing send. I did miss her, but did I want her to know that? Yes, I did.

Gabby: Me too.

Damn, I was falling fast, and it scared the shit out of me.

* * *

An hour later I was sitting in the family room at my brother's house, watching my nephew tear open the presents we'd all brought for him, wishing Gabriella was there to see the excitement on his face. Without thinking, I took out my phone and started a video of him just as he ripped the paper off the comforter, sheets, and Spidey pillow that were all wrapped together. Little Teddy's face lit up with excitement and he squealed loudly. He quickly opened all the others, screaming when he got to the stuffed Spiderman and making his mom open it right then and there. He ran over to where I was still taping him and jumped into my arms.

"Thank you, Uncle Jameson!"

I laughed, holding him on my knee as I flashed the camera at him again. "You're welcome, buddy, but can you do me a favor?"

"Yes!"

"Can you wave to my phone and tell Gabby thank you? She found all of these amazing things for you. She even wrapped them."

I wasn't aware of the complete silence that filled the room from the rest of my family as Teddy hollered, "Thank you, Gabby! Thank you, thank you, thank you!"

Laughing, I gave him a hug, pulling him close and winking into the camera with his face right by mine. Then, I shut off the video and helped him off my lap, shaking my head as I watched him run back to the rest of his unopened presents.

Pulling up Gabriella's number, I sent her the video, then a text.

Obviously, I made favorite uncle. Thank you, baby. For everything.

I'd just sent the text when my brother called across the room, "Did you just send a video of my son to some chick, asshole?"

I glared at him. "No, I just sent a video of my nephew to my woman, so she could see how excited he was with his presents she took the time to get for him when I was unable to." I shrugged, glancing back over at Teddy. "She was worried he might not like them or might already have them. I don't like her worried."

"Your woman?" my mother asked, walking over to sit on the couch beside me. "I didn't know you were seeing anyone, Jameson."

"We just met," I admitted, looking back down at my phone when it vibrated.

Gabby: Aww, look at that adorable face. Your nephew is pretty adorable, too. I'm glad he liked everything. Thank you for sharing.

"Jameson?" I looked up at my mom, whose eyes were glued to the phone in my hand. "I'm confused. You weren't seeing anyone when I spoke to you before you flew out to meet with that guy a few days ago."

"I told you, it's new."

46

"How new?"

"Very," I said, looking down when my phone went off again.

Gabby: I don't know if I will make it over tonight. If I do, it will be late. Luna is having daddy issues.

I burst into laughter, unable to hold it back. Ignoring whatever my mom was saying, I typed back: **No worries, baby. Family comes first. Always. A word of advice?**

Gabby: Yes, please.

If she cares about him, it's important to accept him as he is. If she has made it this far with him, she obviously is interested in that part of him and the role that comes with it. She needs to care enough to accept herself as well and know all of you will too.

As I waited for the reply, I was suddenly aware of how quiet it was in the room. I looked up and glanced around to see all eyes on me. "What?"

"I've never seen you so happy," Jenni said, her hand going up to her mouth as she looked at me in shock.

"I'm always happy," I denied.

"Not like this," my mother whispered, with tears in her eyes.

My phone vibrated, and I hesitated before looking at the text that came through.

Gabby: You think she is afraid to accept the role of a Little?

I think she knows what she wants, baby, but I think she is afraid of what others will think if they find out.

No sooner did I send the text, than my phone rang. I answered it immediately, knowing it was her. "Hey, baby."

I heard my other sister-in-law, Maryanne, gasp. Not only had I never talked to a woman in front of my family before, but I'd never even talked *about* one. Me calling one baby in front of them was a huge thing.

"That's just ridiculous, Jameson Hughes. I love my baby sister. She's my best friend. I would do anything for her. All of my other sisters feel the same way. Why would we care what kind of kinky role-playing theme she likes to play with her man? She's a damn idiot if she thinks I care about that."

I chuckled, shaking my head when my brother Toby's eyebrows shot up in question. They were all standing around me now, close enough to hear the conversation because my phone was up loud, and Gabby wasn't trying to be quiet.

"I didn't say you would, did I?"

"No, but if you know better, then why would you think she doesn't?"

I wasn't sure how to explain that to her. It was just a gut feeling I had. "Talk to her, okay, Gabriella? Let her tell you how she feels and go from there."

"I'll tell her she's an idiot, is what I'll tell her," Gabby grumbled, and I laughed again.

"I would wait until she talks to you first."

Gabby sighed loudly and then changed topics. "So, Theodore liked his presents?"

"He loved them."

"Ask her not to show the video to anyone, Jameson," my brother cut in. "I don't want my son's picture to be flashed all over the internet. It isn't safe."

I heard the worry in Toby's voice, and I hated that I was the one who put it there, but it also pissed me off that he thought Gabby would share something like that with the world.

"You tell her yourself," I snapped, putting the phone on speaker phone. "Gabby, my brother's worried about you sharing Teddy's video with the media."

"He's my son, dammit," Toby shot back. "It's my job as his father to protect him. I don't know who Gabby is, and you said yourself you just met."

"No, you don't know her, but you know me," I said. "You should trust me."

"It's okay, Jameson. He's right, he doesn't know me. And we

did technically just meet, even though my mother has worked for you for over five years now. However, to set his mind at ease, Mama signed a confidentiality clause with you when she accepted your contract, and everyone in our company has signed one for my mother's business. Which means, legally I cannot share personal information of any form with outside sources regarding any of her clients."

"I'm sorry, Gabriella," Toby said quietly. "I didn't realize that."

I hadn't thought about it either, but she was right. If she did share anything about me or my family with the media, I could sue. It didn't mean I wasn't still pissed at my brother.

"I understand, Toby. I'm sure you've had to deal with things like this in the past, and you don't know me, so I completely get why you would worry. I've deleted the video. Thank you for sharing it with me, though, Jameson. It was a bright light in an otherwise difficult day."

"Difficult?" I asked, not liking the sadness I heard creep into her normally happy voice. Quickly taking the phone off speaker, I stood and moved away from my family. "What's wrong, Gabby?"

"Nothing," she whispered softly. "I'm just worried about my mama. I hate seeing her this way, and not being able to do anything about it."

"Come over tonight, baby. I don't care what time it is."

"I have to work tomorrow," Gabriella whispered.

"Bring your laptop. You can log onto my wireless and use the office space upstairs."

She was silent, and for a moment, I worried that maybe I was pushing too hard. Finally, she asked, "Are you sure you don't mind? I could work, and then clean your house, and then have dinner ready when you get home."

My chest filled with a warmth I'd never felt before, and my hand went up to rub over my heart. "That sounds perfect. I'll see you tonight."

"See you then. But, Jameson?"

"Yeah, baby?"

"Don't ever expect me to call you daddy. Just because my sister wants to call her man that, doesn't mean I ever want to call you that, no matter our age difference."

I threw my head back and roared with laughter, not even trying to contain it. Gabriella was one of the sweetest, kindest, funniest people I knew, and I was really looking forward to getting to know her better.

"No? What if I want that," I teased, stopping in front of a bookshelf and staring at it blankly.

"You don't," she said with complete confidence. "You like to be in control, you like acting like a caveman sometimes, but you aren't into anything where I would have to call you Daddy. Now, ropes and handcuffs may be a different story. I haven't had time to figure that out yet."

Just the thought of my woman in handcuffs was enough to get my blood pumping. Only the thought of my entire family standing just a few feet away while they waited for me to end the call kept my dick at half-mast instead of allowing it to become fully erect.

"The second one," I said quietly.

"Interesting," was her response. "That was my first guess."

I closed my eyes and grinned, then said, "I need to go, Gabriella. My family's waiting to grill me."

She laughed, a loud, carefree laugh that could be heard through the phone and around the room. "Do you think Toby would videotape that for me?"

I glanced back at my brother and my grin widened. "Yep, I'm pretty sure Toby would love to tape that for ya, woman, but it isn't going to happen."

"Too bad, big papa. I better let you go."

I about choked when she threw out that name. No part of me was on board with it. "Gabby?"

"Yeah?"

"As funny as that was, it's not going to work."

She sighed, and I could just imagine her shaking her head. "Okay, honey, I will have to come up with something better."

"See you tonight."

"See you soon, Jameson, and thank you for the advice earlier."

"Anytime, baby."

I would be counting the hours until I had her in my house again—in my bed. I had no idea how I could feel like this after just two days, but I decided I wasn't going to fight it. No part of me wanted to.

CHAPTER 9

Gabriella

IT WAS ALMOST midnight before I was able to break away from home and go to Jameson's house. After quietly letting myself in, I made my way up the stairs to his bedroom. Setting my overnight bag and briefcase on the floor by the dresser, I walked over to the bed and stared down at the man that I was quickly losing my heart to.

He was lying in bed with the covers off, one arm flung up over his head with nothing on except a pair of black boxer briefs. A light smattering of hair covered his chest, with a small, mouthwatering path leading down lower toward where those briefs hid what I really wanted to see.

He was asleep, soft snores filling the room, but the pose he was in was so sexy, I couldn't stop myself from slipping out of my clothes and crawling up on the bed with him. My body ached for him, my breasts full and heavy, my skin heated with arousal. I wanted his touch, but more, I wanted to touch, taste, and explore him.

On my hands and knees, completely naked, I leaned over him and licked at first one nipple, then the other, before I began to follow his treasure trail with my tongue from just below his chest, down to the waistband of his underwear. Grasping them in my hands, I pulled them over his cock that was already thickening, over his thighs, and down his legs, tossing them to the floor.

"Damn, baby," Jameson growled, resting his hands on my shoulders, "you sure know how to wake a man up."

"Just *my* man," I purred, my tongue going out to swipe over the tip of his dick, then swirl around the head before encasing as much of his length in my mouth as I could. He was big. Hard and thick enough, I could only take about half of him before I had to pull back up, stroking the head with my tongue again, then sucking him back in.

"Fuck! Gabriella!"

Jameson's hips bucked, pushing his cock even further into my mouth, and I moaned when he tangled his hands into my hair and held me still. He pulled out slightly, then pushed back in slowly, taking control and feeding me his dick.

"Yeah, baby," he ground out, as he did it again. "Just like that. Relax your throat and take it. All of it."

I wasn't sure what he meant, but I tried to do what he said. It was difficult at first, and I began gagging around his length, but then I caught on. I moaned, giving him what he wanted, my hands roaming over his abs and up his chest as I did.

"Fuck yeah, Gabriella," he groaned, as he thrust into my mouth again, giving me even more of his cock. I did what he asked and took it all. My pussy spasmed with excitement when he growled, "Feels so good, baby."

I'd never been a huge fan of doing what I was currently doing, but with Jameson, it was different. Everything was different. I loved it because he was loving it. That, and it was hot as hell the way he took control. I was so turned on, dripping wet with pleasure and anticipation.

"Need to be inside you," Jameson growled, a shudder running through his body. "Need to feel your hot, slick, wet pussy surrounding me. Mine. All mine."

God, I loved it when he talked to me like that. No one had ever spoken to me the way he did during sex. Possessive, growly, dirty talk that set a rush of wild lust racing through my veins.

"Come up here, baby. I want you to ride me."

I moaned, my body trembling with desire. I wanted that too. So much.

Jameson pulled out of my mouth, his hands going to my waist to guide me up his body. I went willingly but made sure to rub against him the entire way, shivering as my nipples ran over the coarse hair on his chest.

His hands went to my hips, and he was lifting me up and over his cock, then sliding me down on it. He went slowly, allowing me time to adjust to the thickness. Steadily, inch-by-inch, he filled me, leaving me breathless when he was finally all the way in. It was just as good as the first time he was inside me, if not better, because this time I was on top, and it felt as if he went even deeper.

I placed my hands on his chest, bracing myself as I moved my hips, sliding up, then back down, taking all of him. Slow. Deep. Perfect.

"Yeah, baby. You are so ready for me," Jameson groaned. "So fucking tight and wet. Love the way you feel."

"Me too," I gasped, unable to get anything else out as he thrust up, bottoming out. Rearing up, he captured one of my nipples, sucking it deep in his mouth. I gasped, my nails digging into his chest as I cried out his name.

His hands went to the round globes of my ass, and he squeezed, then I felt the sting of his hand as he slapped one cheek. It was the most erotic thing I'd ever had happen to me in bed, and I felt my pussy spasm, a gush of liquid coating his erection. Letting go of my breast, he growled, "Move, baby. Ride my cock."

"Oh god, Jameson," I moaned, doing as he asked. No, as he demanded. Soon, his hands were at my hips, helping me, guiding me into a rhythm that he met, thrust for thrust.

"So fucking good, Gabriella," he groaned, a shudder running

through him. "Never felt anything as good as your pussy surrounding my cock."

As the pressure began to build inside me, I moved faster, unable to stop myself. I was chasing that orgasm that was just out of reach, needing to feel it consume me, the way it had the night before.

Jameson moved a hand, reaching between us to find my clit with this thumb. "Come for me, baby," he ordered, as he thrust deep inside me, again and again. "I want to feel that sweet pussy contracting around my cock. So fucking hot and wet. Come, Gabriella."

His words set me off, and I screamed as my orgasm swamped through me, my fingernails leaving marks on his chest, branding him as mine. It was just as good as I knew it would be, but turned out even better.

"Gabriella!" he groaned, as he came, his hands tightening on my hips as he pulsed deep inside me, coating my insides with his cum.

I collapsed against his heaving chest, my arms sliding up around his neck as I nuzzled my face into his throat. His arms went around me, holding me close, one hand gently stroking down my back. Being where I was, in his bed, in his arms, felt so right.

I closed my eyes, fighting back tears at the thought of losing all of this in a few weeks when Jameson decided it was time to move on. I would have to have one of my sisters take over cleaning his house and studio when that happened because there was no way I would be able to watch him move on into someone else's arms. No, I would be moving back to New York. Far away from him and the pain I knew I would feel. But, for now, I was going to hold on tightly to what we had for as long as I could.

Jameson

I LAUGHED SOFTLY as I glanced down at the note on my desk for what had to be the fiftieth time that day. My woman was in cleaning the night before and had left me a message that said 'Dinner at seven. You bring the meat; I'll do the rest.' She'd signed it with a heart beside her name, the way she always did with all the cute notes she'd left beside my calendar.

It had been just over a month since I found her delectable ass leaning over my tub—a tub we'd shared several times since then, and I'd never been happier. She was still working her full-time job, while cleaning for me on the side, but she'd stayed with me every night since the day of Theodore's birthday party. I'd even given her a room down the hall from our bedroom for an office, and a place to park her car in the garage.

My grin widened. *Our* bedroom. I liked that. And, basically, it was ours. Gabby had a couple of drawers in my dresser, along with some clothes hanging in the huge walk-in closet. Makeup was spread out on the counter in the bathroom, along with other girly things. Her shoes were on the mat by the front door, and a jacket in the hall closet. There were bits and pieces of her all over the house, a place that was finally starting to feel like home. I knew she hadn't moved everything from her mother's place, but the majority of it was there. Where it belonged.

I loved going home and having her greet me with her big, beautiful smile and bubbly personality. Not to mention that sass she threw around all the time. If I had my way, she would never leave. New York would be a fond memory, and nothing more. I hadn't talked to her about it yet, but I was planning on asking her to move in permanently. Soon. We may not have known each other long, but it was long enough for me. I knew what I wanted, and I wanted Gabriella Reyes.

"I have those VIP tickets you requested, Mr. Hughes."

I looked up to see Henry hovering in the doorway, watching me with a small smile on his face. My staff knew about Gabriella, even though they'd never met her. Considering there hadn't been a Saturday meeting since that first Saturday after I met her, they were all thrilled that I'd found her.

"Thanks, Henry." Rising, I walked over and took them from him, clapping him on the shoulder. Seven backstage passes to Rebellious Dynasty. My woman didn't know it yet, but she was about to be introduced to not only her favorite band but also to the people in my life who meant the most to me. My family.

"You're welcome, Sir. Hope you all have a wonderful time."

I hoped so too. I was a little nervous introducing my woman to my mother, brothers, and their wives. Not because I wasn't ready for that step in our relationship, but because I'd never brought anyone home for my family to meet before. Ever.

After Henry left, I took out my phone and sent Gabriella a quick text.

Change of plans, baby. Put on something sexy. We're going out tonight.

It didn't take long for her reply to come through.

Gabby: How sexy? Hint of skin sexy, or tear my clothes off halfway through the meal sexy?

Fuck me. As much as I wanted the second one, I didn't want to be hard as a rock all night long in front of my mother.

How about something in between?

Gabby: How much time do I have?

Glancing at my watch, I grinned.

I will be home to pick you up in three hours. Be ready.

Gabby: You got it, Big Pimpin'.

Gabriella had been trying for weeks to give me a nickname, and while they were all hilarious, I denied them on the spot. Every single time.

No.

Gabby: Papa Bear.

No.

I could see the bubbles going, showing she was going to send another one over, and shot out a quick text before she could.

Better get moving, baby, unless you want me to redden that ass when I get home.

I waited, my eyes glued to the screen, wondering what she would say. I meant it as a joke, but Gabriella always gave as good as she got, never failing to put a smile on my face.

Gabby: In that case, I will make sure to be late. I love the feel of your hand on my ass... no matter the reason.

Reaching down, I rearranged my hard cock in my slacks, grunting at the thought of bending my woman over and giving her what she wanted. Unfortunately, it was only early afternoon, and I had a meeting with my managers in fifteen minutes.

I paused, my eyes going to the door, then back to my phone, a slow grin appearing. I was the boss. I made the rules. It was Friday. If I wanted to cancel a meeting and log off early, there was no one to stop me.

On my way.

Gabby: Really?

That ass is mine.

It took me five minutes to shut down my computer, tell Henry to cancel the meeting, and leave the building. I was home within twenty.

I found Gabriella waiting for me in the middle of our bed on her hands and knees, her bare ass in the air. My clothes were off in record time, and I was on the bed behind her, running a hand down the silky skin of her back and over one perfectly rounded butt cheek. When she moaned softly, I brought my hand back, then snapped it forward, connecting with her ass, loving the way she cried out my name. I did it again, then rubbed my hand over where the pale skin was turning a light pink, before giving the other cheek the same attention. Soon, they were both a pretty pink color. The sight of it was erotic as hell, and I had to grab my cock and squeeze to hold off the orgasm that was already building up, threatening to explode.

"Jameson, please," Gabriella moaned, coming out in a low, sensual tone that had pre-cum instantly leaking from the tip of my shaft.

Placing a palm in the center of her back, I pressed lightly, pushing her down until her cheek met the cool sheets and her shoulders rested on the bed. "You are so beautiful, baby," I rasped, as I slipped a hand between her legs, cupping her sex and sliding two fingers inside to see how ready she was. My fingers came out drenched, and I brought them up to my mouth to lick them clean. "So good."

"Jameson!"

Moving forward, I grasped my cock in my hand and guided it to her soaking wet entrance, rubbing the head of it through her juices before sliding deep inside. Her hot channel enclosed around me, squeezing me tightly, and I couldn't stop the groan that rose from deep within my chest. Gripping Gabby's hips, I held her tightly as I began to thrust in and out. It was no slow claiming. It was hard, fast, and almost out of control. The sight of her round, pert ass had set me off the second I walked in the door, and I knew I wasn't going to last long.

"Baby, I'm going to come, and I need you with me."

"Yes!" Gabriella gasped, rising up slightly on her elbows and leaning her head back. "I need your lips, Jameson. Please!"

If my woman wanted my lips, that's what she was going to get. Reaching out, I wrapped my hand around her thick hair and held her still while I slammed my mouth down on hers. I devoured her, licking, biting, sucking at her full, luscious lips, while the entire time I was pounding into her slick heat. Finally, when I felt my balls draw up and knew I was about to come, I tore my mouth away and pulled on her hair, giving her that bite of pain I knew she loved when we had sex.

Gabriella screamed long and loud as her pussy clamped down on my cock like a vise, pulling my orgasm from me. My body went taut, and I held stiff for a moment, before I unloaded inside her. My chest heaving, I stayed like that for a long moment, feeling her contracting around my length, squeezing every last drop of cum from me.

Finally, I leaned down and kissed the side of her neck softly, rubbing my hand over her head gently, before lowering us both to the bed. I held her close, her back to my front, while I stroked a hand down her side. "You okay, baby?"

She nodded, pushing back into me. "Yes, but I think we should stay home tonight. We could eat some leftovers, make some popcorn, snuggle on the couch, and watch a movie."

I chuckled, nuzzling the side of her neck before kissing her bare shoulder. "We could, but then you'd miss out on your surprise."

"Nothing could be better than this."

"No?"

"No," she whispered. "Being here with you is all I need."

My heart stuttered to a stop in my chest, then started pounding at her words. She would never know how much they meant to me. She had absolutely no idea what my plans were for the night, but she didn't seem to care. All she wanted was... me. That was something I'd never had.

My heart filling with a love I was having a hard time conceal-ing. I rested my forehead against her shoulder. "As wonderful as that sounds, we have dinner plans at six and a concert to get to by eight."

Gabriella froze, before turning over to look at me, her hands coming up to grip my arms. "A concert?"

"Yep, with backstage passes."

Her gorgeous brown eyes widened in wonder, and she whis-pered, "Rebellious Dynasty has a concert downtown tonight."

I smiled, kissing the tip of her nose. "How would you like to meet the band, Gabby?"

Gabriella's face lit up, and she squealed in excitement. "Yes, please!"

"There's just one catch," I said, pulling her closer. When she cocked an eyebrow in question, I grinned. "We are going to dinner first, just the two of us, then we are meeting my family at the concert. I got them tickets, too."

"Your family?" she asked in confusion, before leaning back slightly from me.

"Yeah, Gabby. It will be my mother, Toby and Jennie, and Chandler and Maryanne. I want you to meet them, and they are excited to meet you."

"You want to introduce me to your family?" Gabriella whis-pered, her brow furrowing as her hands tightened on my biceps.

I nodded, trailing my fingers gently over her cheek, loving how soft her skin was. "Yeah, baby. You mean a lot to me."

"I do?"

I frowned at the uncertainty and hesitation in her voice. "Yes, Gabriella, you do."

A small smile appeared, and she whispered, "You mean a lot to me too, Jameson."

I closed my eyes, lowering my forehead to rest it against hers. She'd thrown me off guard there for a moment, making me wonder if all the emotions I was feeling were one-sided. Hell, I was still worried, but I wasn't going to say anything more right then. I was afraid if I did, I would send her running back to New York, which was the last thing I wanted. Up until a few minutes ago, I could have sworn she felt the same way. Now, I wasn't so sure.

CHAPTER 11

Gabriella

I WAS EXCITED to meet the band, but was also extremely nervous about several different things. High on that list was being introduced to Jameson's family. Up until this afternoon, I thought he was just looking for a fling. Someone to entertain him for a few weeks until he was ready to move on. While I wasn't a 'love them and leave them' type of girl, I'd been willing to accept that just so I could have a few memorable days with the man I'd wanted for so long. As much as it hurt, I was prepared to let him go when he was ready, even though no part of me wanted to. I'd fallen hard for him over the past few weeks, easily losing my heart to the man who now consumed my thoughts day and night.

I was afraid to get my hopes up that I wouldn't have to let him go, but there were obstacles in the way. For one, my life was in New York. I could change that easily enough. I had nothing holding me there, except for possibly a job I wasn't in love with, anyway. Everything I wanted was here in California. Which brought me to my second obstacle. Jameson. Was he looking for something long term? Did introducing me to his family mean the same things to him as it did to me? Was it as important as I thought it was?

"You okay, baby?" Jameson asked gruffly, as he helped me out of the car at the concert venue. He'd driven right up to the front door, valet parking. I didn't even know they offered such a thing, but I guess when you are a hotshot producer and were going to watch one of your bands play, you received more perks than others.

Looking up into his dark brown gaze that was full of concern, I felt my breath catch in my throat at the sight of something else in his eyes. He wasn't just worried about me, there was more there. Kindness, caring, and if I was reading his expression correctly... there was at least the beginnings of love.

That hope that had sprung up earlier in the night began to blossom in my chest, on the verge of exploding, as I raised a hand to rest it lightly on the neatly trimmed beard that covered his strong jawline. Giving him a tender smile, I whispered, "Yeah, honey, I am now."

The corners of his mouth turned up into a slow, sexy smile as his head began to lower. Then his lips were on mine. I stiffened when there was an explosion of lights around us, jumping when Jameson's arm slid around my waist, holding me tightly. Swearing softly, he slammed his car door shut, handed someone his keys, and quickly ushered me through the front doors, away from all the cameras and people yelling questions at us.

"I'm sorry, Gabby. I wasn't thinking about the media being here."

"What were you thinking about?" I teased, trying to calm him down as I increased my steps to keep up with his long strides.

"I should have taken you in the back way," Jameson snarled. "Kept you away from all the fucking vultures. Protected you from their bullshit. Because I didn't, we are going to be front page news tomorrow."

I kept quiet as he ushered me to the back of the concert hall and into a small room where others were waiting. I'd never seen him so upset, and the fact that it was over his worry for me made my heart warm. He was vibrating in anger, still swearing under his breath, and suddenly I couldn't stop the laughter that bubbled up and escaped. Glaring down at me, he ignored the looks of confusion on the faces of the people I assumed were his family as he snapped out, "What the hell is so funny, woman?"

"You," I said, throwing my head back and laughing louder.

"You think it's funny that I'm pissed?"

I shook my head, reaching up to rest a hand on his chest. "No, crazy man. I think it's funny that you are going all caveman over some pictures."

"Dammit, Gabriella, you don't understand. You have no idea how the media can twist things around. There is no such thing as an innocent picture with them. Tomorrow morning, we are going to be splashed all over every social media outlet there is. Some will question who I'm with, some will find out your name and dig up everything there is to know about you and share it with the world. They will tear into our lives because they have nothing better to do with theirs."

"It's a good thing I have no secrets then, isn't it?" I said lightly. When he just glared at me, I leaned up and kissed him gently. "Jameson, no part of me wants my personal life plastered all over the place for everyone to see, but it isn't worth getting so upset over. It happened; it's done. We can't change it or control the actions of others."

"From what we are hearing, you must have just been subjected to the famous part of Jameson's life," a woman interrupted, moving across the room toward us. She was tall and slender, with short dark hair with a slight hint of silver throughout. Her kind, brown eyes sparkled at me as she went on, "He tries to protect all of us from it."

"There's nothing wrong with wanting to protect the people I love," Jameson growled, pulling me closer and lowering his head to bury it in my neck, a gesture he had done many times and always turned my insides to mush. Then I froze as the implications of what he'd said sank in. He'd just grouped me in with his family, the ones he loved. Did that mean what I thought it did? Was he saying he loved me, too?

"Jameson," I started tentatively, raising a hand to slide it into the hair at the nape of his neck, holding him close to me, "you can't protect us from everything in life. I'm not an idiot. I knew something like this was a possibility when we started dating. It doesn't matter what they post tomorrow, or the next day, or the day after that. They can say whatever they want. I am not ashamed of any part of my life. All I care about is you and what you think or feel."

I felt a shudder run through him, and then he raised his head to look at me. "It's never mattered before," he said gruffly. "It does with you. *You* matter."

"Very eloquently put, Big Brother," a man joked from across the small room, where he held a petite blonde in his arms.

"I thought it was perfect," I whispered, my gaze holding Jameson's, before I leaned up and pressed a kiss on his jaw. "Now, how about we table this discussion for later when your entire family isn't listening, and enjoy the rest of the night?"

A slow grin spread across Jameson's face, and he found my lips with his. The kiss was short and hard, conveying the depth of his emotions before he pulled back and muttered, "Good idea, baby. Ready to meet my family?"

Laughter filled the room as I glanced over at the others and grinned. "Well, that was one way to break the ice."

* * *

The concert was even more amazing than I thought it would be. It was the first real live one I'd ever been to, and I was glued to my seat the moment Rebellious Dynasty took the stage. They were exciting, charismatic, and knew how to enthrall an audience. The best part was that Jameson never left my side.

As soon as it was over, we were led backstage, where we quickly used the restrooms and then were taken to the band's dressing rooms. I stood close to Jameson as he introduced me and his family to Xander. I'd wanted to meet the attractive singer for years, but all I could do was stammer a hello when he greeted us.

"Hey there, gorgeous," the lead guitarist said smoothly, coming over to stand beside Xander and holding out his hand to me. "I'm Brett. It's always nice to meet a beautiful woman."

I felt Jameson stiffen beside me, and I took a step closer to him, enjoying the hint of jealousy that was coming off him. Slipping one of my hands in his, I reached over and shook Brett's with the other. "It's nice to meet you, too."

Jameson let go of my hand to slide his arm around me and pull me close, and I immediately melted into his side. I loved the way it felt when he held me, and I wanted him close to me.

"This is Micah. He plays drums. Gavin's on base guitar, and Jayse plays both guitar and keyboard, depending on the song," Jameson said, nodding to the men as they each reached out to shake my hand, then greeted Jameson's family.

"It's wonderful to meet all of you," Maryanne gushed. "We've seen you in concert several times, but never made it backstage."

"I don't know that we ever would have met them if it wasn't for Gabby," Chandler teased, winking at me. "I'm pretty sure Jameson would do just about anything for his girl, including introducing her to all of his rock stars."

"Which reminds me," Jameson cut in, guiding me over to sit down on a small couch next to him. "My woman has one of the most beautiful voices I've ever heard. While she tells me she has no interest in a recording deal, I was hoping you might share a few songs with her. I'd love to hear your vocals together."

"Jameson, no!" I protested softly, clutching his arm tightly. "They just got done performing. I'm sure they are exhausted."

"Actually, we'd be honored," Xander said, grinning widely as he walked over to grab an acoustic guitar that was resting in a stand on the other side of the room.

"We'd never turn down hearing a beautiful voice," Jayse cut in, as he grabbed another guitar and then moved a chair to set it down next to the couch, sliding into it.

"Oh, no!" I whispered, my hand going up to rest against my throat as I shook my head adamantly, looking over at Jameson in a panic. "I would rather just listen to all of you."

"I would love to hear you sing, Gabby," Jameson's mother, Rebecca, said, giving me a radiant smile. "My son obviously knows a good voice. He signs them all the time. I'm sure he would sign you in a heartbeat if you agreed."

"But I don't want that," I whispered, my eyes going to Jameson's imploringly.

"I know, baby," he said, kissing me gently, right there in front of everyone. "Just humor me. Please."

Slowly, I nodded, biting my bottom lip nervously as I glanced around the room before looking back at him. "For you."

Jameson's eyes lit with happiness, a wide grin spreading across his face. He kissed me one more time before nodding over to Xander.

The first song was a slow one. One they'd released right after they signed with Wicked Chords. I knew it from beginning to end and was able to sing the entire thing with them. Letting my eyes drift close, I shut out everything and everyone except the music and guitar chords that were strumming through my body. I was so caught up in the lyrics, I was unaware of when Xander stopped singing with me.

When the song came to an end, I opened my eyes to find the room quiet, and everyone staring at me in awe. My heart began to race with nerves, but Xander immediately put me at ease when he started playing a second song. One that wasn't his but was meant to be sung with both male and female vocals. I smiled, moving closer to Jameson as I lost myself in not only that song, but three more after it.

Finally, Xander set his guitar down and walked over to kneel in front of me. "Girl, Jameson is right. You can sing. Why wouldn't you want a record deal with a voice like that? Hell, I know I speak for the band when I say, you can sing with us anytime."

I felt my face flush a dark red at his praise, and I found Jameson's hand and clutched it tightly as I shrugged. "I don't know, I just don't. That lifestyle isn't for me. I love singing, but it isn't a passion of mine," I tried to explain. "If I had to do it all the time, I probably wouldn't enjoy it as much."

"I can respect that," Xander said, nodding slowly. "Consider it an open invitation, though. You ever want to hop on stage with us and show the world what you got; we would love to have you."

Snuggling close to Jameson, I smiled when the rest of the band spoke up, adding their agreement. "Thank you," I whispered, smiling at them. As happy as it made me that they all enjoyed my voice, and as much as I appreciated their invitation, I knew I would never collect on it. I had no desire to be in the limelight with all eyes on me. Singing in the privacy of my own home was enough for me.

CHAPTER 12

Jameson

MY JAW CLENCHED as I stared at the newspaper I held. A picture of Gabriella and me was front and center on the first page. The caption read 'Cinderella and her Billionaire Prince'. It went on to state how a woman who worked for the company that cleaned for Wicked Chords had snared the owner himself. The last line read, 'Is she after his heart... or his money?' One of the same things I'd been wondering since Gabby and I met weeks ago.

The article wasn't any different from numerous other ones that I'd seen since the media captured us on camera three nights ago. It brought all my old insecurities racing back, and had me once again questioning my woman's true feelings for me. It pissed me off because no matter how many times she'd proven herself, that damn small twinge of doubt was still there. I couldn't seem to let it go.

"Why do you keep reading that trash?"

I looked up as Gabriella walked into the kitchen, setting her purse and briefcase down on the counter. She was dressed in a white button-down blouse with a straight, navy-blue skirt that stopped just above her knees and black heels on her feet. Her hair was pulled back into a sophisticated bun, and she wore a dainty, thin gold necklace with a matching bracelet. Briefly, I wondered where she was going, before my mind shifted back to the article I'd been reading.

Taking a sip of coffee, I glanced back down at it. "I don't like the things they are saying about you."

"Well, it isn't going to change, no matter how much you read it."

"Why don't you seem to care, Gabriella?" I bit out, tearing my eyes from the newspaper to look at her again, standing all calm, cool, and collected in front of me while I was anything but. "They have this same shit plastered all over the place, and it doesn't seem to bother you at all. Why is that?"

"Because, Jameson, we both know it isn't the truth. I'm not after your money. I don't care about what kind of status you might hold in the record industry, because I have no desire to land a recording deal. I know that. You know that. That should be all that matters." She paused, her eyes narrowing on me. "You *do* know that, right?"

Did I? My hand tightened on the paper as I stared at the article headline, then back at the woman I'd given my heart to. *Had that been a mistake? Was she using me?*

"Jameson?" Gabriella whispered, taking a step toward me. "You do know that, right? You don't actually believe that crap the media is spreading, do you?"

I stiffened, hating the hurt I heard in her voice. The first sign that any of this bothered me.

"I see," she said, tears glistening in her eyes. "A part of you does believe it."

"Gabby..."

Shaking her head, she held up a hand. "No, don't say another word." Grabbing her purse and briefcase, she turned and stalked over to the door that led to the garage. Glancing back, she ground out, "After the other night, I thought you understood how I feel, Jameson, and I really thought you felt the same way. At first, I figured you were just out for a piece of ass. And even though I have never been that woman in my lifetime, I wanted to be with you, any way I could have you. Even if it was for just a few days. But then we started building something special... at least, I thought we were." A tear slid down her cheek as she continued, "I've always paid my own way. I've bought groceries and other things for what I was starting to think of as my home, too. Hell, I bought your nephew's birthday presents. I've never asked you for a penny. I have my own money; I don't need or want yours. But I gave you something very precious to me, something I've never given another man. I gave you my heart, Jameson, but now I'm wondering if in your eyes I will always be just that poor girl who scrubs your toilet and floors."

My hand on the newspaper tightened as she turned and walked out the door. She was right, I realized. She'd bought Teddy's presents, and I'd forgotten to pay her back. She'd never said a word. Slowly, I glanced around the kitchen, noticing the things she'd added that made my house look like a home. The sunflower mat in front of the stove that matched the pictures now hanging on the wall and the placemats on the island where I sat.

Slowly, I stood and walked into the living room, where she'd added more of her touch. Pictures, knickknacks, a throw blanket on the back of the couch. It all screamed Gabriella. Why hadn't I noticed it before? Or maybe I had, but I just hadn't acknowledged exactly how much of a change she'd made. I'd been too stuck on the fact that she might still leave me, but those weren't the actions of a woman who was still thinking about moving back to New York.

Making my way up the stairs, I went to the room Gabriella now used as an office. There were books in the bookcase that had sat empty since I bought it, along with pictures of her family. An image of the two of us in a white frame with hearts in all four corners was on the corner of her desk, one I hadn't seen before.

I ran a finger down the edge of the frame as I stared at the way

Gabriella was looking at me, a radiant smile on her face, eyes full of emotion. I knew exactly when it had been taken. A selfie I'd posed for but had never looked at afterward. You couldn't miss the love my woman felt that the camera had captured.

Swallowing hard, I stepped back, letting my gaze wander around the room again. Her laptop was gone, which meant she hadn't been planning on working from home today. Home.

Raking a hand through my hair in agitation, I stomped out of the office and to our bedroom. I cursed loudly when I looked in the closet, seeing a small portion of the closet that was now over-flowing with her things. It looked like she'd been shopping recently *with her own money* because she hadn't asked me for any. She never asked me for money. Ever.

My feet dragged against the floor as I walked over to the chair I'd put by the window. A chair specifically arranged so Gabby had a place to read at night. The stress I held in my body as I sat heavily down in the seat was fucking with my head. No matter how you spun it or which way you looked at it, I always came to same conclusion. This house felt emptier now than it ever did any time before I met Gabriella. She changed me—my outlook, my life, my home. She made it ours, never asking for anything in return, only being here because she wanted to be with me. I should've never let my insecurities get to me the way I did. None of this had ever been Gabby's fault... it was mine. Always mine.

And that's when I knew I'd royally fucked up.

CHAPTER 13

Gabriella

THAT SON OF A BITCH, I thought for what had to be the hundredth time as I stood just outside the Blake International Resorts Hotel looking out at the waves of water in front of me. It was located off Ocean Beach in San Diego, not too far of a drive from the place I'd begun to consider home until less than an hour ago.

I couldn't believe Jameson would feed into the rumors that had been circulating since Friday night. Hell, we'd even talked about it. We'd known it was going to happen. It had been inevitable, considering both of our backgrounds. What I hadn't considered was the fact that he might actually start believing them.

"So, what do you think, Ms. Reyes? Are you interested in the position?"

I would have been all over it just this morning, before my discussion with Jameson. I'd wanted to stay in California, stay with the man I loved, so I'd been watching online for job openings. The minute I saw one for a marketing manager at the resort, I applied. I was surprised when I got an interview, as I knew I didn't have the amount of experience they were looking for. Of course, it helped that Luna was dating the son of the resort owners. I found out he made some calls that got me where I was right now.

"Ms. Reyes?"

Inhaling deeply, I turned from the beautiful panoramic view in front of me to face the man beside me. My mother raised her girls to fight for what they wanted. I wasn't going to give up. I would not run. And dammit, Jameson Hughes was about to find out that he was not going to push me away, no matter how screwed up in the head he might be right now.

"Yes, Mr. Mason, I am very interested."

"Great!" Mr. Mason replied with a satisfied grin, accepting my hand when I held it out to him to shake. "When can you start?"

"I'd like to give the company I work for now two weeks, so any time after that."

"We look forward to working with you, Ms. Reyes. We will email you all the forms that need to be filled out so you can have them ready when you start."

After saying my goodbyes, I headed back to my car. I'd been planning on working from my mother's that day so I could check in with my sisters, but plans changed. Instead, I found myself driving back to the mansion, my anger ratcheting up the closer I got.

By the time I parked my car in the garage next to his, I was livid. Slamming the door behind me as I entered the kitchen, I glared at the newspaper that was still sitting on the island next to a half-empty cup of coffee. My chest was heaving. I was so furious, as I stalked through the living room and up the stairs, looking for the person I wanted to take my anger out on.

I found him in the bedroom, sitting in the chair he'd gotten just for me, his elbows on his thighs, his head in his hands.

"Jameson Hughes!" I started stalking over to stand in front of him. "You are a damn idiot. You listen to me, and you *hear* me! I love you! Not your money, not your image, not your damn company. I love *you*! And you are going to have to figure your shit out, because I just accepted a job here in San Diego, and I'm not leaving just because you can't..."

He was out of the chair before I could continue, his lips on mine, his arms banded tight around me. I gasped, and he took full advantage, his tongue pushing past my lips to find mine. Finally, he pulled back, resting his forehead against mine as he rasped. "I love you too, baby, so fucking much. I don't care about anything except you. Fuck the media and what they think. I know you, trust you, and I love every single part of you."

"You do?" I whispered, all of my anger leaving me in a rush. "You... love... me?" I had to pause between each word, emotion clogging my throat as his words sank in. He'd never said those words to me before, but I felt them now, deep in the heart that was pounding inside my chest, surging with the love I felt for him in return.

"Yeah, baby, I love you."

My arms went around his neck and I held on tightly as I let his words flow through me. He loved me! He trusted me! Jameson Hughes loved me, and in my heart, that was the only thing that mattered.

CHAPTER 14

Jameson

I STARED down at the dark blue velvet box I held, wondering if it was too early to give it to the woman I'd fallen deeply in love with. We'd been together three months now, and I couldn't imagine my life without her in it.

Gabriella had proven to me over and over again that she was with me for *me* and not what I could offer her. She didn't want fame and had no interest in my money. Hell, she still grumbled when I tried to buy her anything expensive.

She still cleaned at the studio, not allowing anyone else to do it. She cooked, cleaned, and took care of our house. I discovered that she loved to decorate for any season, and right now it was decked out in everything Thanksgiving. I couldn't wait to see what she did for Christmas. I looked forward to finding a tree to put up with her and had already started shopping for all the presents I planned on putting under it with her name on them.

I now spent all my free time with her. Even going so far as to change my work schedule, handing over some of the duties I'd held onto for longer than necessary to others in my company, which meant I was normally home by no later than six every night.

I glanced over at the framed newspaper article on the side of my desk. It was a beautiful picture with a very well-written article about two people from different backgrounds finding each other. I was so grateful for a positive spin on things. It had earned the author an exclusive interview with Rebellious Dynasty. Gabby's family was mentioned, but spun in a very positive light, avoiding the Cinderella theme others seemed focused on.

Gabby was the one who cut the article out and framed it. I found it waiting on my desk two days after it appeared online. She loved it, which meant I loved it.

My phone vibrated, and I looked down to see a text from Gabriella.

Gabby: Might be a little late tonight. I'll make dinner when I get home. XOXO.

Home. I loved that it was now *our* home.

Take your time. Be safe.

Opening the box, I looked inside. A large, princess cut, two-carat diamond ring sat inside, the band adorned with smaller diamonds that went halfway down on both sides. I'd gone into the store with the intention of purchasing something bigger, but this one caught my eye, and I knew it was perfect.

I glanced down at the screen when my phone went off again, smiling at the message.

Gabby: I always am, honey.

Honey was the only pet name she called me that I'd ever approved of. I liked it, even if I didn't let on to her how much. She still occasionally threw out other things that made me laugh, things she knew I would never go for, but when she called me honey, it made my heart beat just a little bit faster because I always hear how much she cared for me in that one word.

Seeing that it was almost two in the afternoon, I decided now was the perfect time to set my plan into motion. Too soon or not, it was happening tonight. I couldn't wait any longer to find out if the woman I loved felt the same.

After placing a quick call to a florist downtown, I let Henry know I was leaving for the day and went to put my plan into motion.

IT WAS after six when I finally got home from work. After parking in the garage, I hurried into the house. Dropping my purse on the island in the kitchen, I kicked off my high heels and picked them up, rushing through the living room to the foyer.

I stopped dead in my tracks when I saw the stairs leading up to our bedroom. They were covered in light pink and dark red rose petals, and even from where I was standing, I could tell they led down the hall.

"What the hell?" I muttered, my heart catching in my chest before it started to race.

Grasping my shoes tightly, I made my way up the stairs, stopping at the top to turn and look back down at them.

"So beautiful."

"I'm glad you like them."

I spun around, one hand going to my mouth as I stared at the man I loved with all my heart, standing at the end of the hall in a black tux.

"Jameson?"

He held out a hand, and I slowly walked toward him, placing my free hand in his when I got there.

"You look beautiful," he said, his eyes raking over my outfit before coming back to me.

"Jameson? What's going on?" I whispered, glancing into the bedroom and letting out a soft gasp. The rose petals made a path into the room and then covered the bed.

Letting go of him, I walked in and took a slow look around. There was a bottle of wine chilling in a bucket of ice on a stand in the corner, and more rose petals going into the bathroom. The things were everywhere. There were also vases of dark red and pink roses all over the room, along with several candles that looked as if they'd been recently lit.

"Jameson?" I whispered, turning back to him, dropping my shoes to the carpet when I saw him down on one knee in front of me, clasping a dark blue velvet box. "Oh my god."

"Baby, come here," he said, holding out a hand to me. Slowly, I crossed over to him and placed my hand in his. My heart was pounding frantically, and I clutched tightly to him as I watched his eyes soften and a small smile form on his lips. "I know we haven't known each other long, but to me, this feels like the beginning of forever. I love you, Gabriella Reyes, more than anything in this world. Will you marry me?"

My chin trembled as tears filled my eyes. "You want to marry me?"

"More than anything."

Slowly, I dropped to my knees in front of him, cradling his face in my hands. Tears spilled over, gliding down my cheeks as I smiled at him. "I want nothing more than to be your wife, my love. I love everything about the life we are building together and can't wait to see what the future holds."

"Really?"

I nodded. "Really." My eyes went to the box he still held in front of me. "I love you so much. Yes, I will marry you, Jameson Hughes."

Before I could say anything else, his arms were around me, his lips crushing against mine. After a moment, he pulled back and opened the box, lifting out the ring and sliding it on my finger. It fit perfectly. It was huge, with several smaller diamonds surrounding it. "So beautiful."

"I'm glad you like it."

My brow furrowed as I looked up at him. "How did you know my ring size?"

"Luna," he said with a grin.

"Of course." I laughed, holding my hand out in front of me so I could see the ring better. It was stunning, and the light from above shone off it, making it sparkle brightly. "I love it, honey. Thank you."

"I love you," Jameson said, before standing and pulling me up with him. "Now, you have two minutes to take those clothes off before I strip them from you."

"What?" I asked, looking up at him in surprise. Where the sweet man who just proposed to me had been just a second ago, now stood a growly, very turned-on man with a hard cock pressing against the front of his tuxedo pants.

Walking over to the dresser, he opened one of my drawers and reached in, turning around to hold up a pair of light pink furry handcuffs. My face flushed in embarrassment, and I let out a giggle I couldn't hold back.

"You found my toys I bought when I went shopping with Luna a few months ago."

Reaching back into the drawer, he pulled out a purple vibrator. "We'll talk about your toys later, baby. Right now, I'm more interested in playing with them. Clothes off and on the bed."

I giggled again, stripping quickly before climbing up onto the large bed. "How do you want me?"

"Any way I can have you, my love," Jameson said, as he began to strip his tie off.

I watched as he removed his clothes, my gaze roaming over every part of him. Laying back on the pillow, I held my arms out as he got up on the bed, and crawled up my body, kissing and licking his way from my belly button up to my mouth. He thrust his tongue past my lips at the same time he entered me with his cock. I moaned loudly, lifting my legs and wrapping them around his waist.

I felt the clasp of the handcuff go around one wrist, then it was raised above my head and hooked to the bedframe behind me.

"Mine," Jameson growled, the fingers of his other hand threading with mine as he lowered his head to capture my nipple in his mouth.

"I love belonging to you," I whispered, arching up into his body, pressing his thick cock deeper inside me. "I love you."

"I love you, and being yours too, baby."

Note From The Author

Make sure and visit my website for information on all of my books, and to sign up for my Newsletter where you will receive all of the latest information on new releases, sales, and more!

Website: **http://www.dawnsullivanauthor.com/**

I would love to have you join my reader's group, Author Dawn Sullivan's Rebel Readers, so that we can hang out and chat, and where you will also get sneak peeks of cover reveals, read excerpts before anyone else, and more!

https://www.facebook.com/groups/AuthorDawnSullivans-RebelReaders/

Looking For More Billionaires?

Be sure to check out the rest of the series!

1. Maid For You by ChaShiree M.
2. Maid To Tempt by Annelise Reynolds
3. Maid For Me by Dawn Sullivan
4. Maid To Desire By S.E. Isaac
5. Maid For Him By Chelle C. Craze
6. Maid To Hate by DC Renee
7. Maid Of Mine by M.K. Moore
8. Maid To Love by KL Fast & Roxy Lynn Coming Soon!

About the Author

Dawn Sullivan has a wonderful, supportive husband, and three beautiful children. She enjoys spending time with them, which normally involves some baseball, shooting hoops, taking walks, watching movies, and reading.

Her passion for reading began at a very young age and only grew over time. Whether she was bringing home a book from the library or sneaking one of her mother's romance novels to read by the light in the hallway when she was supposed to be sleeping, Dawn always had a book. She reads several different genres and subgenres, but Paranormal Romance and Romantic Suspense are her favorites.

Dawn has always made up stories of her own, and finally decided to start sharing them with others. She hopes everyone enjoys reading them as much as she enjoys writing them.

Other books by Dawn Sullivan

RARE Series

Book 1 Nico's Heart

Book 2 Phoenix's Fate

Book 3 Trace's Temptation

Book 4 Saving Storm

Book 5 Angel's Destiny

Book 6 Jaxson's Justice

Book 7 Rikki's Awakening

White River Wolves Series

Book 1 Josie's Miracle

Book 2 Slade's Desire

Book 3 Janie's Salvation

Book 4 Sable's Fire

Serenity Springs Series

Book 1 Tempting His Heart

Book 2 Healing Her Spirit

Book 3 Saving His Soul

Book 4 A Caldwell Wedding

Book 5 Keeping Her Trust

Sass and Growl

Book 1 His Bunny Kicks Sass

Book 2 Protecting His Fox's Sass

Book 3 Accepting His Witch's Sass

Book 4 Chasing His Lynx's Sass

Chosen By Destiny

Book 1 Blayke

Book 2 Bellame

Alluring Assassins

Book 1 Cassia

Dark Leopards East Texas Chapter- this series is written with three other authors

Book 1 Shadow's Revenge

Book 7 Demon's Hellfire

Book 10 Taz's Valor

Magical Mojo

Book 1 Witch Way To Love

Book 2 Witch Way To Jingle

Book 3 Witch Way To Cupid

Rogue Enforcers

Karma

Alayla

Evalena

Standalone

Wedding Bell Rock

The De La Vega Familia Trilogy (Social Rejects Syndicate)

Book 1 Tomas

Book 2 Mateo

Made in the USA
Middletown, DE
27 June 2022

67851440R00060